Capturing Cora

ROMPS & RAKEHELLS

MADELYNNE ELLIS

INCANTATRIX PRESS

Copyright © 2012, 2014, 2020 Madelynne Ellis. All Rights Reserved.

Cover Art by Madelynne Ellis

Editing by Allison Jacobsen

First published in 2012 by Ai Press.
This edition published by Incantatrix Press 2022.

This is a work of fiction. The names, characters, places and incidents are products of the writer's imagination or have been used fictitiously, and are not to be construed as real. Any resemblance to persons, living or dead, or to events or places is coincidental.

www.madelynne-ellis.com

ISBN-13: 978-1500440190

-Also by Madelynne Ellis-

HISTORICAL EROTIC ROMANCE

Scandalous Seductions
A Gentleman's Wager
Indiscretions
Phantasmagoria
Three Times the Scandal
Her Husband's Lover
The Ghosts of Christmas Past
The Serpent's Kiss

Romps & Rakehells
Capturing Cora
Seducing Sophia
Taming Taylor

Forbidden Loves
The Kissing Bough
Pure Folly

CONTEMPORARY EROTIC ROMANCE

The Black Halo Books
Come Undone
All Night Long
Remastered
Come Together
All Fired Up
Resistor
Come Alive
All Right Now
Reflex
Replay
Revive (due 2020)

MADELYNNE ELLIS

Anything But...
Anything But Vanilla
Anything But Ordinary

Stirred Passions
Cherry Bomb
Black Velvet
Soul Kiss

The Bad Boys of Brit Pop
Crazy Love

Standalone titles:
Dark Designs
Enticement
Passion of Isis
Sharing Adam
Gabriel's Naughty Game
Confessions of a Greedy Girl
Exposure

GOTHIC URBAN FANTASY ROMANCE

Blood Moon
Broken Angel (prequel in Possession)
Prophecy
The Demon Way
Shadow Queen

-1-

A WAGER & A PROPOSITION

SIX YOUNG LADIES, occupied the skittles alley at Rievaulx House yet there was not a single chaperone in sight. This was why Miss Cora Reeve had chosen this particular moment to propose a friendly wager. "For after all," she remarked. "None of us wish to be purveyed like horse flesh for a second season. A little incentive might spur us on in our pursuit of husbands. So, what say we agree that whoever secures the first proposal shall win a little something from each of the rest?"

"Cora, isn't that gambling?" Harriet Cholmondeley asked from her perch atop the old pianoforte stool. Cora's best friend was so petite and doll-like her feet swung inches above the floor. "Are you sure it's quite right? Won't our chaperones be vexed with us? I don't wish to be sent home in disgrace." Harriet's gaze swung fearfully toward the window. Outside on the lawn their chaperones were partaking of tea.

"Well, I don't comprehend the problem with being invited to another score of parties," Biddy, the youngest of the group, remarked. Since her arrival she had been interested more in the accumulation of scandalous gossip than a husband. "I shan't put myself out to secure a proposal. None of the gentlemen here would suit me at all. They are all too fond of themselves and indulging their vices. Lord Swansbrooke spent forty minutes last night reciting the names of his hounds to me. As if I should care that he has one named Horace, let alone three."

Cora ignored Biddy and focused instead upon her dearest friend, whose hands she clasped reassuringly. "What will our guardians care about a few chicken stakes, Harriet? Heavens, I only mean for you to win my hat. None of us are set upon compromising our virtue. Nor do I believe I'd be able even if I were intent on such a thing, with both my mother and Aunt Tessa watching over me." She squeezed Harriet's knuckles and was blessed with a nod of acquiescence.

To Harriet's flanks both Amelia and Persephone also signalled their consent. That left Charlotte, who stood holding her fan like a baton she meant to strike them with. She ticked Cora upon the arm with it. "My concern is that this is not a particularly fair wager. Certain of us are far more advantaged than others, and therefore better placed to win." She shot a look at Amelia. "Given Mr. Hulme's obvious attachment, Amelia is certain to triumph."

Amelia flushed prettily and bowed her head, so

that only the blonde crown which had been interwoven with blossoms could be seen. "I think you overstate my hand. Mr. Hulme is very kind, but I don't believe he sees me in his life in such a permanent way. I'm sure it's only that he feels a little sorry for me."

Kind was not quite the word for it. Attentive was more accurate, perhaps even lecherous, if one were being unkind. Nevertheless, Cora echoed the pooh-poohs of the other women. "Wasn't it Mr. Hulme's influence with Lord Egremont that ensured your invitation?" Amelia had no family to speak of and only a modest living. "How are we supposed to interpret that other than as a sign of attachment?"

Amelia gave a delicate shrug. "I'm not the only one possessed of an admirer. Persephone held court to at least five beaux last night."

"I did," Persephone admitted, though not with any relish. Instead, her attention rested upon the portrait of their host upon the rear wall. Alas, Lord Egremont showed no reciprocal signs of affection. In fact, he was always noticeably absent from the coterie of bucks Persephone gathered.

"Do make sure not to forget Cora," Biddy remarked to Charlotte. "Why, she and your brother are practically married already. One only has to perceive her skill at skittles to know how much time they've spent together, and hardly a minute of it properly chaperoned from what I've heard."

Cora opened her mouth to make a retort, only for Persephone to step regally between her and Biddy. "I believe it's your turn, Cora."

Very well, she'd let that slight go, but only because it was in fact the truth. Tink—or more correctly—Branwell Locke had indeed taught her the art of skittles, alongside horsemanship, dice, archery, and trout tickling, to name but a few of her more unusual accomplishments. She excelled at them all, whereas her embroidery was mediocre and her singing voice akin to a caterwaul. "We're nothing more than childhood friends," she huffed under her breath. "More's the pity."

Cora snatched up the skittles ball. She wasn't sure when over the last few months things had changed so that Bran had stopped being her fond companion and transformed into an eligible gentleman. She supposed it coincided with her formal presentation into society. Maybe it was merely her perception that had changed.

Bran still treated her like a sister.

She longed to be his wife.

He still tweaked her ringlets and ribbed her mercilessly about her sawing laugh. She longed to have him notice her in a different way.

When she gazed at Bran, her breath quickened and she imagined the taste of his merry lips pressed to hers delivering illicit kisses. She longed for the summer days they'd spent scrambling over hills and wading through brooks, and how they might live those days over as lovers if only he felt the same way.

She knew his smile and the mischievous light in his leaf green eyes. Knew too that he bore scars upon his arms from the punishments inflicted by one former schoolmaster and a lump upon his left shoulder from where he'd cracked a bone as a boy. Such insights she'd gleaned over years, but now she seemed cursed to gaze upon him from the near distance with little to no chance of ever being noticed there. Let alone winning any further intimacies.

Bran simply didn't feel the same way.

Determined not to allow bitterness to overwhelm her good humour, Cora dashed forward a few steps, swung her arm back and released the wooden ball, which rolled fast and straight across the glossy floor. It smashed into the pins at the far end of the alley, sending them flying.

Grimly satisfied, Cora dusted her hands, before turning back to her friends and their incorrect suppositions. Only to be greeted instead with stunned applause. Both Charlotte and Persephone embraced her.

"I don't suppose there is time to achieve such mastery in the time we have before the gentlemen join us," remarked the latter.

"We can try," Cora assured her encouragingly.

"Oh good, then I'll take my turn next." Persephone drifted down the room to straighten the pins. Cora drew her teeth over her lower lip. While she could produce a strike, Persephone would make skittles into an elegant art form, even if she never hit a thing. Her friend had always stood out. Her glossy chestnut ringlets made her intriguing among the mélange of demure blondes, and Bran had been one of the bucks paying court to her.

Persephone took her throw, using predictably beautiful steps, only for the ball to roll sluggishly and fail to topple a single pin.

"Use your wrist more," Cora advised, not that she truly believed it would help.

Harriet's attempt impressed little better. Cora stood back to allow Charlotte her throw, since she had also benefited from Bran's past tuition. His sister toppled all but two pins, prompting her to clap in delight. It was only afterwards that Charlotte turned to her thoughtfully.

"Cora, forgive me, but I can't help suspecting that this wager is a plan you've devised with my brother to cheat us of our things. I swear, if he suddenly makes a great show of wooing you, then—"

"He won't. Well... I haven't planned anything. How could you—"

"Haven't you?"

"I never cheat. And Charlotte, we're simply friends. You of all people are perfectly aware of that. Besides, even if Bran did propose, he would only do so in jest. He wouldn't actually marry me." Much as it hurt her to admit that fact. "I'm simply not to his tastes."

"Is that so? I've always observed my brother to be particularly fond of you."

Fond—perhaps! If only that were enough. "If I'm to spend my life with him, I shall want more than fondness." She desired passion and love. She craved his actual touch. "I shall want to be central to his needs."

Harriet tugged at her skirts. "Cora, you oughtn't to dwell upon such improper thoughts. Think of what your mama would say if she heard you."

Cora raked her teeth over her lower lip again. What was so wrong in her thinking of Bran, or any other man, in that way? Where was the evil in admitting her admiration? It seemed unlikely that the Lord God would strike her with a thunderbolt for admiring a fellow's calves or the merry way in which his lips curled, or even for imagining him creeping towards her bed in the dark. After all, how else was procreation supposed to occur? She had grown up in the countryside and wasn't naïve enough to believe in storks or bountiful gooseberry bushes.

If she occupied her nights dreaming of how Bran might touch her in places she'd explored once or twice for herself, then whose business was it besides her own?

More importantly, she absolutely insisted on feeling something deeper than passing interest in her future husband. She refused to be the sort of wife who was confined to the country estate so her husband could make merry with his mistress.

Why should her husband have need of a mistress? Could he not make merry with her?

"Cora!" Harriet barked, making everyone jump.

"Whatever did I do?" Cora made her eyes wide in defence.

"It's what you were thinking that was the problem. I could tell the turn of your thoughts purely from your expression."

"Oh, and what pray were they?" Charlotte asked.

"Nothing I would consider repeating."

Charlotte cocked an eyebrow in a way that reminded Cora sharply of Bran. "That simply makes it all the more intriguing."

"It was nothing. I was merely considering an addendum to our wager. That it has to be a genuine match for the winner to be declared. Hopefully then you won't consider my motivations so suspicious."

Biddy pushed her way into their midst. "Whatever argument you have will have to wait. The gentlemen are here." Almost as she spoke, the doors to the adjoining room were thrown open. Their host, Lord Egremont, led the column of gentleman guests, with Bran by his side.

"I trust you are all well practiced, ladies?" Bran came straight over to their huddle. "Whatever are you all about? Do tell." He took in all their expressions. "You all look deliciously guilty. What can you have been planning?" He cocked an eyebrow just as his sister had just done. "Do say, Cora. You know I can't abide being kept in the dark."

Why did her heart have to flutter so much just from looking at him? Somehow, she managed to keep her agitation out of her voice. "You're mistaken in thinking there is anything afoot. We have merely been practicing."

"They are embroiled in an audacious wager." A smug grin turned up the corners of Biddy's mouth.

Treacherous imp! Cora stiffened. Bran didn't need to know their business any more than any of the other gentlemen. Secrets were not something he was overly good at keeping. More importantly, while the wager was meant light-heartedly, the matter of finding themselves husbands was absolutely serious, and Bran would only make fun of them. She really didn't think she could bear to have him laugh at her when it came out that the plan had been hers.

"They—" Biddy began.

"It's nothing."

"If it were nothing, Cora dearest, you wouldn't look so alarmed." Bran ticked her lightly upon the forearm. "I don't suppose this wager has anything to do with skittles, perhaps?"

"More to do with you," Biddy piped up, refusing to be quelled.

Bran closed his eyes a moment, transforming his expression into one of quiet appraisal. "Is that so? You do realize we're to be a team for the event, so it may not be to our advantage to be too competitive with one another."

"Oh, this has nothing to do with the skittles."

"Be quiet, Biddy!" Charlotte stamped on the little imp's foot. "For heaven's sake hold your tongue for once."

"Am I to conclude that you are in on this too, sister dearest?" Bran adjusted his stance so that he stood closer to his sister. Standing side by side the family resemblance between Bran and Charlotte became completely apparent. Same narrow elfin nose set above plump, sensual lips. Although Charlotte's features were sharper, both siblings possessed the same oval shaped faces, each with a dimple in their left cheek that appeared when they smiled. Naturally, Bran stood a good head and shoulders taller. His hair was a softer blond too, lightened by time spent out-of-doors in the sun. The latter had also left him with dark freckles across his brow and the bridge of his nose. Charlotte, of course, never directly exposed herself to the sun for fear of the same affliction.

"It's only a little fun between us women, brother."

Bran folded his arms across his chest and waited for her to elaborate. Charlotte defiantly raised her chin, only for Harriet to capitulate instead.

"Um," Harriet gave a delicate cough. "We all agreed that whoever receives the first offer of marriage shall win a selection of gifts from each of us. See, there's no harm in it. We haven't done anything wrong."

"Oh, Harriet!" Cora murmured. She loved her friend dearly but did wish that Harriet wasn't so easily compelled. Now all the men would know about their venture and it would turn into a posturing competition. If any of the beaux were considering making offers, they'd now be competing in order to win their prospective bride a prize. That or they'd be fleeing in the opposite direction.

"My dear, Miss Cholmondeley, I never thought such a thing in the first place." Bran turned to spy the room over his shoulder. "Swansbrooke," he called. "You ought to hear this given your reputation with the ladies. If you make a proposal, you could win your chosen belle a prize."

"But only if she accepts," Cora insisted.

Lord Swansbrooke rubbed his gargantuan nose thoughtfully. "One hopes that one's prospective wife loves one for oneself and not the bounty he might provide. I shan't be bending onto one knee until I'm certain my advances will be wholeheartedly welcomed. Now, I wonder, Miss Cholmondeley, if you would partner me for the skittles game?"

Harriet left on Lord Swansbrooke's arm. Charlotte followed a moment or two later, swept away by Persephone's brother, Paris. Persephone and Amelia both excused themselves, announcing they would take a stroll around the gardens with Mr. Hulme instead.

Cora remained beside Bran, her head held high, unwilling to make an excuse to leave, despite her fear that he'd further pursue her part in the wager. Her stomach laboured like a butter-churn each time he seemed ready to say something, but for some indeterminable reason, Bran seemed to change his mind and remained quiet after all.

In the past they'd never had such trouble communicating with one another. Why was it so difficult now? What's more, they seemed to have lost their knack for wordless communication too. As children they'd always known the other's thoughts. Now, she struggled to properly judge his mood.

It was not until the game was underway that

Bran finally enquired, "I trust that you would actually like to win."

"Of course."

He stood so that his face lay half in shadow. One pale gold lock fell in an unruly spiral over his brow. "You don't wish to let Miss Cholmondeley triumph, or perhaps Miss Townley?"

"Heavens, no." Well, she wouldn't mind if Harriet won, but she had no intention of aiding Biddy with anything.

"Good. Very good." Bran fell silent again, which only emphasized the gulf that had grown between them. "Cora..." He took hold of her hand. "Ah, it appears to be our turn."

Confused, Cora took her throw. She felt Bran's gaze upon her back and could make no sense of it. Had he been trying to tell her something? Had he—heaven forbid—found someone he wished to wed?

Her ball struck the wooden men so hard it was a wonder they didn't splinter. As it was, they leapt out of their places and scattered.

Behind her, applause broke out. Over the top of which she heard Bran cry, "Yes!" in triumph. Cora turned in time to see him snatch a floral display off the windowsill. Then as she stared at him perplexed, he launched himself towards her, falling onto his knees so that he slid across the polished floor. Bran came to rest with a bump at her feet.

"Cora," he began, as he had done at the start of her turn. Then he cleared his throat. "My dear thing, my darling, Miss Reeve—Cora." He stretched the stolen posy towards her, clearly meaning for her to accept it. This was all a little theatrical. He'd seen her make a strike on countless occasions.

"Will you be mine? Will you marry me, my most majestic lovely? It's obvious to me from that strike that we're meant for one another."

What? What was he saying?

A broad grin stretched across Bran's face, thinning his plump upper lip, but making his merry green eyes twinkle.

Heat seared her cheeks. "Don't," she murmured, realizing his posturing had drawn everyone's attention. "Don't say things that you don't mean." Couldn't he see the hurt he caused?

"You did say you wanted to win." He pushed the posy a fraction higher. When she didn't accept it, he bounced up onto his feet. "Shall we jump the broomstick together, Cora, and make merry in the hay?" He linked his arm with hers and turned a full circle.

"Why are you doing this?"

"You did say you wanted to win."

"The skittles, aye."

Bran stopped jigging and thumbed his jaw as he ruminated on her reply. "Ah—" He sobered, but only a little. "So, you didn't intend me to propose?"

"I didn't intend for you to do anything." She spoke loud enough to make sure everyone heard. Charlotte would not have grounds on which to accuse her later. She'd had no hand in his gesture.

"Then your answer?" He picked apart the bouquet until only a few flowers remained, which he tucked into the ribbons that criss-crossed the front of her dress.

"No."

What else could she say? He didn't mean it.

"You don't genuinely mean for me to become your wife. Please don't speak to me like this again." She wasn't at all sure she ever wanted him to speak to her again.

Blinking back tears, Cora fled the room.

-2-

OF MINT & PEA-POD WINE

"**D**AMN THE GODDAMNED woman to hell!"

Bran slumped onto the marble bench at the front of the mock Corinthian folly and swore vehemently at the sky, the fountain, and whomever goddamn else happened to overhear him, which, as it happened, turned out to be the blasted woman's mother. He scowled, causing the mouse-like Mrs. Reeve to pale down to her furbelows and shuffle backwards into the towering fronds of foliage.

"It's nothing to get your rump in a toss over," he mumbled at her retreating silhouette.

How the woman had come to produce such a romp of a daughter quite confounded him, then again, he'd heard more than one rumour to the effect that Miss Cora Reeve was in actuality the issue of her father's mistress, Tessa de Lacy rather than that of his timid, bespectacled, wife. Considering the colouring and demeanour of the three women, and after the outrageous handling he'd been subjected to, he could well believe it. Tessa de Lacy notoriously reduced grown men to tears, something Cora had brought him near to.

Genuine! If he'd sewn his heart onto his sleeve and then ripped the whole out at the seams he couldn't have been more sincere in his affections. He thought she of all people would realize that.

As for Mrs. Reeve, well, she ought not to be so nosy if she didn't care for his cursing. Nor should she follow him into the shrubbery after dark. Didn't she realise there were sufficient rakehells about tonight to form an army? He stared at the dark hollow amongst the overgrown lavender into which the woman had retreated, and only when he was quite sure she had gone did he allow his head to sag forward into his hands.

Cora, Cora... What was he to do? This moment ought to have been one of rambunctious declarations and all round celebratory hell-raising. Instead, it was about as exciting as watching a donkey race the day after the Derby.

He and the delectable Miss Reeve were a perfect match. Admittedly, he'd been slow in realization of that fact, but familiarity did tend to make one a little blind. He trusted Cora was suffering from a similar affliction.

The woman was an absolute hoyden for turning him down. She hadn't even given it a moment's thought, and all because of that dreadful wager she'd made with the giggling bunch of ninnies he was supposed to be wooing.

As if he'd make a mockery of something so

important to her, to his, to their future happiness. He'd half a mind to go and find her again and shout out the damn proposal while swinging from that ridiculous oversized chandelier Egremont had recently installed in the family drawing room. Except, if one flamboyant gesture had already failed, what chance had a second?

If she turned him down again, laughed, he might find himself contemplating a deep dive into the river rather than a simple trip to the far end of the blasted garden.

"Cora, I want you. Not any of your preposterous friends!" he bellowed at the night sky. Why did she have to be so blinkered?

Bran shuffled on the stone plinth, the cold already beginning to seep into his bottom, so that the skin had become numb. He settled his back against the privet and looked for inspiration among the stars. The search didn't do him any good, just resulted in leaves in his hair and an uncomfortable recollection of having his knuckles rapped by his tutor for failure to identify Pegasus. Damned Greek horse looked more like an oversized kite than a foal bearing thunderbolts. He still wasn't sure that he had the constellation. Was it that big square, or the off-centred diamond?

The crunch of approaching footsteps set Bran onto his feet. While he hoped it would be Cora, his ears told him well enough that the tread was too deep. Cora moved like a spring breeze over water. When she danced, her body rippled next to his, and he floated with her whenever her skirts brushed his thigh. The approaching figure moved like he was wading through horse manure with his best Persian slippers on, which at least narrowed things down a bit as to who it might be.

"Tink, are you here? Where are you, I can't see a thing in this blasted dark." The cry reached him over the hedgerow.

"Here, Hugh."

His robust friend ambled into the sparse clearing before the folly a moment later, with his arms stretched ahead of him. "Ah, good, I did strike out right. Thought I heard you muttering a minute ago. I've brought you a tipple to quell your humours. Figured you might need one, after all the to-do with Miss Reeve." He winked at Bran, before slumping down onto the stone plinth. "It's a dreadful sticky mess you've waded into. Your sister seems to believe you were being genuine." The incredulity in his voice suggested Hugh, like Cora, believed otherwise. At least Charlotte knew him well enough to recognise his plight. Charlotte had seen enough of his home life to know he hadn't always been the court jester. Nope, by twelve he'd had nearly all his humour beaten out of him.

"I was sincere."

"Ah! You do realize that you didn't exactly sound it? Not coming on the tail of that wager." Hugh raised the glass in his hand to his lips, only to pause before drinking. He offered up the liquor to Bran instead. "You'd best be having this. I find it's the best cure for when they don't take you. A nice jig with the faeries soon sets you straight again, and you realise she just wasn't the one."

Hugh would know. Polly Perkins had made it rejection number six last Wednesday eve. Probability said sooner or later one of the dames he asked would bite. It wasn't as if Hugh didn't have plenty to offer: a nice Cotswold estate, a pedigree dating back to the Norman Conquest and a very warm and gracious heart. What he didn't have was a pretty or in any way handsome face. Hugh had a nose on par with an elephant's, which coupled with his beady sparrow-like eyes made him look more caricature than man, and completely overrode the Swansbrooke name.

"Best you forget it, Tinker and try for another one. You're not short of admirers. The right one will come along."

Bran heaved a sigh though his nose. Relationship advice from the most rejected man in England, just what he needed. "I'm not giving up on her." He didn't even want to contemplate a shared existence with another woman. Besides, in his heart, refusal aside, Cora was already his. He'd been wandering about with her image in his head and another pressed to his heart too long to yield after the first hurdle. He couldn't, wouldn't let her escape.

"What are you going to do?" Hugh asked after they'd spent a minute or two staring into the darkness. He offered up the drink to Bran again, who took it, and a mighty gulp.

The liquid left Bran's mouth again almost immediately. "Jesus and damnation! What is that muck?" He wiped the residue from his lips with his coat cuff, although the sharp and tart taste continued to burn his tongue.

Hugh offered him a sympathetic shrug and patted him on the back to help with the expulsion. "That'd be Reeve's Special Mint and Pea Pod Wine. Fierce, ain't it?"

It was certainly something, although fierce wasn't top of the list of adjectives he'd have used. God-awful and muck featured rather more prominently, along with dreadful and piss. "Who the devil looks at a pea pod and thinks, I know, let's turn it into wine?"

"I believe Reeve has a fascination with watching the maids shell the peas, and well, waste not want not..." Hugh seized the glass and drained the remainder, giving a sigh as it went down. "But you know, Tink, you never did answer me. What will you do? She's not a flighty creature. She's one of the stubborn ones, and if she's said no, I can't see that she'd change her mind."

She hadn't precisely said no. She'd simply not believed him serious. Although, Hugh had a valid point, the minx would probably think a second proposal a mere continuation of the same theme.

"All suggestions welcome," he said.

Hugh peered forlornly at the empty glass. "What does the father say?"

"Reeve? He told me he'd be only too delighted for me to take her off his hands, and could I please make it prompt so as he can retire to his sheep farm in Cumbria before the shearing starts. Also he'd like to get back to the business of tupping his mistress rather than being flounced around London like a prize bullock with golden cobs. There was a tad more than that, something involving a haberdasher, but I didn't catch all of it."

"So, you've his blessing."

"If you can call it that."

Hugh dug his elbow into his thigh and rested his chin upon his open palm. "I don't know," he said. "Not short of stuffing her in a sack and refusing to let her out until she agrees. Can't see how else you're going to change her heart."

He didn't want to change her heart. He wanted her to sit and listen and acknowledge the fact that the offer was real. If she still said no, then so be it. He'd have to assume the love between them was exclusively on his part, and that perhaps no amount of courting would change that. First though, he needed to get her to listen and realise he wasn't making a mockery, but that he genuinely did love and admire her. No other woman would ever accept him in the way Cora would, or be so comprehensively involved in his life.

"You know," he remarked, while swiping his hand through the undergrowth. The heads of several flowers toppled on to the path. "The sack idea's not such an appalling concept."

"Bran, it's a truly revolting idea. No woman's going to want you after you've tied her in a sack."

"Then for heaven's sake give me an alternate way of getting her alone."

"You don't need me to tell you that. You're adept

at it. What was it you were saying was your favourite game the other week, that variant on hide and seek?"

"Hugh!" Bran threw his arms around his friend and smacked a kiss upon his cheek. "Of course, you're a genius."

Hugh cocked a brow. "So, you're going to suggest hide and seek?"

"Nope." He bundled his friend off the bench and back onto his feet. "You'll have to suggest it. If I announce it, it'll just raise suspicions. Come along now, back to the house."

-3-

OF BUFFETS & GAMES

"**B**UT WHAT IF he was serious?"

Cora tapped the tip of her fan to her pout and glared at her friend. She could only see Harriet's back for the other woman was huddled behind the privy screen adjusting the ribbon ties of her stockings. Cora didn't even want to contemplate that possibility. Better that she accepted it as the insincere nonsense it had been. "He made me look foolish with all that overzealous posturing and his declarations." Her gaze strayed from Harriet to the nosegay of foxgloves and baby's breath Bran had pinned to her bodice. Annoyed, she tore it off and cast into the nearby grate. "He only did it because Biddy told him of our contest. He wouldn't even have thought of it otherwise."

"I don't know, Cora. Doesn't it say something that he was at least prepared to attempt to win you a prize? As for his posturing... He has always been one for flamboyance."

Cora shook her head refusing to let herself

believe. If Bran had stripped her naked, stuck a number on her rump and paraded her around the room like a prize heifer she wasn't sure it would have hurt so much, but to dangle something she wanted so badly before her like that... that hurt. She clenched her fists tight as the splinter of shock that still remained embedded in her heart worked itself loose.

He simply couldn't have been serious.

She'd seen how he looked at Tessa de Lacy, all wide eyed and slack jawed. He'd never stared at her like that. Although to be fair, there weren't many men who didn't stare at Aunt Tessa in that way.

Some folks said she and Tessa looked alike, but Cora couldn't see it. Tessa had hair the colour of honey, like buttercups scattered across a meadow. Cora's hair was more brassy and held none of the light, nor did it curl quite so prettily.

But what if he had been serious? And he took her at her word, and never did address her thus again. Might she have just ruined everything?

"Are you done?" she asked Harriet. "We ought to get on with this business of hiding. They'll start seeking soon."

"I'm done. Where shall we go?" Harriet emerged with her wide apple-blossom and gold skirts fanned around her. "I thought I might take the window seat next door, the curtains are of a similar fabric, so I might blend in."

Cora's gaze dropped to her own outfit, deep ocean-blue with sprays of turquoise, emerald and jet. She'd be accused of not trying, which would only make her mother upset. "Go ahead, I'll find somewhere else."

Harriet scampered off, and Cora turned in the opposite direction. She slipped across the corridor and stepped around the hounds in the dog-parlour, making her way to the concealed buffet. The cubbyhole contained only a few dusty knickknacks, which were easily pushed into one corner. Having folded her voluminous skirts around her, she climbed inside and inched the door closed behind her.

There wasn't much air in the cupboard, and it was fusty and dark. Cora spent the first few minutes pressed to the door frame, sucking in breaths from around the gap in a state of nervous anticipation. When after what felt like five or more minutes had passed, she grew impatient, shuffling her feet, and finally sagged against the rear wall with her eyes closed.

When Bran had got down before her holding that posy, she'd so desperately, desperately wanted it to be real. A wry smile claimed her lips. The sting of tears in her eyes soon followed. She refused to let them fall. Listening to him say all those things she'd dreamed of hearing him say and knowing he meant not a single word of it, hurt like a tear in her chest. Even now, she could hardly catch her breath at the thought of it. Only for a split second had she contemplated saying yes. Accepting him was what she wanted, but she loved him too much to bind him to match he didn't genuinely desire. He had to want her every bit as much as she wanted him.

The sound of movement in the room beyond

provoked an irritated snort. "Oh, just find me. Let this be over with, so that I can retire," she muttered under her breath. She'd plead a headache, and no one would miss her. The racing pulse in her temples certainly resembled a migraine, even if it was her heart that was really afflicted.

The motion ceased and she supposed maybe it had only been the dogs shuffling about.

Damn you, Branwell, for not loving me back. Why couldn't he love her back?

The buffet door opened, prompting a small gasp to escape her throat. Bran smiled on spying her, but instead of hollering out that she was found, he squeezed into the cupboard beside her.

Cora pulled herself up straight.

Little light penetrated the cupboard, but enough to see his ruffled forelock and the red-gold glint of his lopsided queue. "What are you about?" she demanded.

"Hiding. Weren't you listening? The seekers are to hide alongside the hiders, until we're all squashed together and everyone is found."

"Oh!" If she'd known, she'd have opted for a curtained window bay likewise little Harriet. "Were there others following you?"

Bran grin broadened so that she saw the gleam of his teeth. "No. Most of them headed into the other wing."

So, they were alone.

"I needed to talk to you, Cora." Bran reached out and tugged one of the ringlets that spilled over her shoulder. He let go when she squashed herself against the wall to avoid the contact, and the ringlet sprang free, falling to rest on the swell of her bosom.

"If you're referring to your earlier tomfoolery, I've already heard enough for one night." Her words sounded strangled as she forced them out past the toxic lump in her throat. The tears she'd worked so hard to suppress prickled her eyes again. One escaped and rolled down her cheek, but she quickly brushed it away. "You've already embarrassed and ridiculed me enough. Can't you see when to stop? Oh, confound it. Let me out of this cupboard. It's improper we being together like this, and you know it."

She drove into him, leading with her elbow, but Bran didn't move an inch, other than to groan over the impact.

"Cora... Sweet pea, I have never ridiculed you. Not ever."

"You're still doing it now, and don't call me that. You know I hate it."

"Do you?" he mused, pressing finger and thumb to his lips. "You wore them in your hair to the Faringdale's masquerade, do you remember? Who was it you were supposed to be, Mary Mary? You're certainly being contrary. Cora, I thought we understood one another."

"I know you mean well, but..."

Bran pressed his index finger to her lips. "Stop. Retrospectively, I admit my timing was ill-conceived." His voice quavered a little as he spoke. "I ought to have waited until we were alone, but you're damned near impossible to pry from your group. Oh, Cora. I never intended to be disingenuous, but rather romantic. I love you. Why shouldn't I declare it before everyone else?"

Cora squinted at him, her thoughts in tumult. He sounded so serious. If only she could see him clearly enough to tell if he still sported that playful pout.

And if he didn't?

Then maybe she didn't want to see… Gosh, he must think her the most ungrateful, appalling romp for refusing him like that. She pushed again at his torso. "Please, Bran, let me out."

"Cora." Rather than moving aside, he crowded her. The taut muscles of his thigh pressed tight to her skirts, so that heat radiated all through her lower limbs. An inferno lit deep in her womb when he leaned closer still and touched her. His fingertips traced the line of her jaw, and his thumb nudged up her chin so that their gazes met.

Bran's eyes gleamed just above hers, onyx dark in the pitiful light. "Don't run. Please don't turn me down a second time in one day. Cora, I love you. I'm an appalling fool for not realizing it earlier. What am I saying? I've known it forever, but I didn't want to deprive you of your Season and your coming out ball."

"Oh, Bran, as if any of that ever mattered."

He swept his thumb upwards and gently brushed across her parted lips. Cora's pulse began a flighty dance. She hung on his every word. Sweet heavens, was he about to kiss her? She parted her lips, willing him forward, to take what she so desperately wanted to give, while at the same time, her fingers clawed so that her nails dug into her palms. She ought to be strong and remain aloof. Only, she so much wanted his love it was impossible not to strain towards him.

Bran's warm breath mingled with hers. Their lips lay no more than a finger's breadth apart. "I want you, Cora Reeve. I want to do wicked things to you that will make more than this faint heat colour your cheeks. I want to push your legs apart, get down on my knees and whisper that proposal you laughed off into your quim, and maybe once I've made you sob with bliss, you'll finally take me seriously."

Her lower part seemed immediately awash with heat, so too did her cheeks, for what he'd suggested wasn't at all polite. No true gentleman would ever have spoken like that, but Bran had never treated her like a piece of china. He's shared enough ribald jokes with her to know she wouldn't faint just because he'd been lewd.

"I've spoken to your father. He took me seriously."

"He did? You have?"

"Aye."

"Why didn't you say so earlier? I'd have known then. I wouldn't have doubted."

"It didn't seem very romantic to bend down and say that I'd spoken to your father first. It seemed presumptuous, nor did I wish to imply that by speaking to him first I considered you somehow irrelevant, when you're so very, very far from being that."

The buttery slur of Bran's words wrought havoc with her self-restraint. Heavens, if he didn't kiss her soon, she would take the matter out of his hands.

"I want you, Cora. Say yes, because I'm so sorry, but I have—" He touched her cheek. Then one hand slipped into her hair. The other rested against her bodice. "—I simply have to kiss you."

He pressed his tongue between her lips and wakened desires she couldn't put names to, not even images. She clung to him, dizzied by all she was feeling, and in turn he held her back, crushing her body to his. Bran's kiss bore no resemblance to the chaste, powdery and familial brushes of affection she'd been accustomed to. Arousal flooded her body. The rush of blood in her ears drowned out everything else.

A slow tingle rolled down Cora's throat and into her breasts, so that her nipples ached and chafed against the inside of her stays.

She wanted... yearned...

Bran's large hand cupped her face, and his forefinger stroked back and forth over her flaming cheek. "Cora, say it. Say yes."

She strained towards him, balancing on tiptoe to compensate for the difference in height, and initiated the second kiss. To the devil with being wholesome and chaste. Bran was everything she wanted. This close, even insulated by numerous layers of fabric, he literally radiated heat. "Yes," she agreed. "Yes. Yes." To whatever he wanted. To passion and rubbing herself naked against him. These were the things she truly wanted. Not an exchange of vows in a church, but passion and torment and all the emotions that made a person feel alive. Though heaven help her if she wasn't moving into territory she had no experience of.

Bran's hands moved possessively over her bodice. Then his thigh pressed between her legs, rousing an even more dangerous sort of excitement. "Touch me," he whispered. "You don't know how often I've dreamed of you holding me."

Cora released her grip on his shoulders. Daringly, she pushed her hands inside his frock coat. Solid muscles rippled beneath the flare of his waistcoat. Beneath that, yards of shirttail sat tucked into his breeches, which tug as she might, she couldn't quite find a way beneath in order to touch his skin. "I swear you have on more layers than I do."

"Probably more," he agreed. "Though not so many petticoats."

"Oh, Bran." She jabbed him playfully.

In return, Bran drew his kiss away from her lips. He began to tease her earlobe and the very top of her neck. At first, she shied from the sensation. It seemed almost too intense to bear, and made her ache low down in her belly. Then she leaned in to the kiss, craving more, until she literally hung onto him, unable to speak, barely able to stand.

"Do you like that, my sweet?"

"Oh!" Her breath released as a hiss. "Don't stop."

"So, you do like it?" He nuzzled against her hair,

kissed her brow, but didn't return to her neck. He shuffled his feet too, so that he wasn't pressed so firmly against her.

"What is it?" she asked.

Bran smiled. "I'm just growing a little excited too, my pet."

"What do you mean? You mean like the stallions?" Her gaze shot downwards to his loins. Even in the dingy light of the cupboard she could make out the lozenge-shaped hummock distorting the frontfall of his breeches.

Cora's mouth turned dry.

"Don't let it scare you, my love."

"I'm not scared."

That was a lie and they both knew it. Still, she couldn't help but stare at him curiously wondering how it would feel, and how it would look in the flesh.

"You needn't worry. I shan't do anything ungentlemanly."

"Will you not?" Cora gave a nervous giggle, realizing that a hint of disappointment had threaded her response. It wasn't that she specifically wanted to move their relationship forward that quickly. They were in a precarious position, in a closet, after all, and she was hardly experienced in such matters. It was just that... Well, she wanted to touch him, to know him. All of him. There had to be a first time. Why not make it now, while she felt a little daring and a great deal crazy?

"Can I? May I... Bran I want to touch you there." She reached out as she said the words, trying not to think too hard about what she was actually doing. She brushed one fingertip against the ridge beneath his front fall before jumping back as if scalded.

When nothing happened, she wheezed a sigh of relief, and then clamped a hand to her mouth.

"Do that again," he said, grinning.

"I'm not sure that I should."

"Oh! Why is that, Cora?"

"I think you might like it." Her cheeks ached from the grin that stretched across her lips. She'd always deliberately sought to do whatever she shouldn't. Wasn't that the reason why she rode like a fiend and why she could swim and fish and bowl? She'd trusted Bran to teach her all those things, so why not trust him now?

Besides, her curiosity was winning over her sense of fear again.

Bran's breath whooshed into her ear as she settled her palm over his loins. She encompassed his length with the flat of her palm. She didn't squeeze or fondle, simply remained still with the heat of him against her hand.

"How does it work, Bran? Is this the part you'll put inside of me?"

"Dear God," he swore. All the muscles in his abdomen pulled tight. "Cora, you'll be the undoing of me if you say things like that. I think it's time we left this cupboard."

"Wait. I didn't mean to do anything wrong. I just want to be able to please you. You're the one who taught me to ask questions in order to conquer my fears. I want everything to be wonderful between us."

"Yes, but not here, not like this. Not right now."

Cora swore he hadn't meant them to, but his words worked like magic. Suddenly, she not only wanted to see and feel his length properly, she was determined to. Grinning as she did it, Cora slipped open the first button of his frontfall.

Bran's breath hitched. "I ought to stop you right there."

"But you won't."

"Hell, I might."

Cora shook her head. "Just let me hold you. Just for a moment." His second button opened as easily as the first. Only one other button held his breeches closed, but already her impression of his shape was much clearer.

"Woman, you don't know what you're asking."

Oh, but she did. "Branwell Locke, don't you dare become an honourable gentleman now."

~ * ~

Being honourable was very far from Bran's thoughts, as Cora opened the final button of his breeches. He couldn't stop her. Hell, he craved what she was about with every inch of his soul.

Bran's vision had adjusted to the dark well enough to make out her features clearly now, certainly well enough to see her eyes widen. Her perfect rosebud lips parted slightly to release a gasp.

"This isn't the time or place for this," he

reasoned.

She didn't let up, but instead used her fingers and thumb to discover every inch of his cock. When her exploration became increasingly bold, he thanked God that he'd worn his longest shirt, the tails of which met between his thighs and stopped her making direct skin on skin contact. At this very moment, he didn't think he could tolerate that. Hell, that touch of hers would have him spending in no time at all, if he didn't put a stop to it.

Her thumb swept up over the tip of his cock, and the radiance that crackled through his lower half nearly spun him into orbit.

"Cora." Bran clasped her hands in his and raised them so that they were pressed to the wall on either side of her head. Romp that she was, she actually tested his strength. "Minx, I think it's time we got to the business at hand, rather than my business in your hand." He kissed the tip of her nose, then dipped his head and planted two kisses on the luscious swell of her breasts.

She smelled of cinnamon and honeysuckle, and the latter scent reminded him just what he intended to do next—suckle. It was time he gave her taste of what he intended to do to her once he had her in his bed, starting with how he intended to lave his tongue around her nipple and cover her breasts in gentle nips.

"What do you intend to do?"

Wild excitement glowed in her eyes when he glanced up. "Everything you ever dreamed about."

She smiled, showing off a flash of white teeth,

which Bran read as a challenge. "You've no idea what I've dreamed about."

"Then I shall have to go off my very best guesses. If I happen to miss anything, I'm sure you'll inform me." He planted another kiss upon the upper swell her breast, and then released one wrist so he had a hand free to work with and traced the scooped neckline of her bodice.

Cora's breathing quickened. Her lacy fichu barely covered a thing, so that if she leaned forward even an inch or if he removed a couple of pins then the already glorious sight before him would transform into a heavenly one.

Bran reached for the fastening only to discover it a fake, and that the front of her bodice had been tacked into place.

Not to be thwarted, he tugged at the stitching until it came loose. Then he pushed his palm beneath the satin and the edge of her stays. Her bare breast filled his palm, pleasantly weighty, the skin smooth and soft. Her nipple peaked and crinkled tightly against the centre of his palm.

"Bran?" She trembled slightly as he lifted her breast free of the fabric.

"Yes, my love." He took a moment to explore her pulse point with his lips before weaving a path lower and tracing his tongue lightly over her nipple.

She stiffened and then gasped as he sucked, and whatever it was she'd meant to ask him became lost in a sea of mewls.

How quickly the tide of events had turned. Little more than an hour had passed since she first refused him, and now he intended to make a far grander gesture than the first in order to secure her promise. He meant to bring her to fulfilment, and whisper his pleas at the exact moment she reached climax. He wanted to hear her scream her reply loud enough for every goddamned guest in Rievaulx House to hear it. And then, once she had properly said yes so that everybody knew it, then and only then, would he let the ache in his loins find relief. First of all though, he had to pray that Swansbrooke led the other hide and seek players on a merry dance in the other wing for long enough for him to see this through.

Keep them away, Hugh, he silently wished. *Do so, and I'll do whatever it takes to help you find the right woman too.*

~ * ~

Speechless, Cora let her head fall back against the cupboard wall. Bran's touch sapped all her strength. Her limbs were jelly-like, hardly able to support her weight. A fever ran between her nipples and her puss and tied them together in knots of fire. She'd never guessed it would feel like this. Oh, she'd dreamed of holding Bran in her arms, even of having him come creeping into her bed , but as for the actual sensations invoked, she'd never even come close to imagining them. They were sweet and sharp, and they made her want... She didn't really know what it was that she craved, only that Bran was definitely the one to deliver it.

While his mouth remained at her breast, his

hands had begun wandering. He held her about the waist while he smoothed his other hand over the fabric of her skirt, and then he began hitching it as though to find a way beneath.

"Heavens, is there any need for all this frippery? There's enough fabric here to re-curtain my bed." Despite the complaint, laughter rather than vexation filled his voice, and he had no problem in finding his way beneath the various layers of petticoat. His big palm touched her leg where her garter clasped her stocking top. Then, he knelt and his scalding breath stirred the curls of hair upon her muff.

Cora stiffened in fearful anticipation. Her breath seemed trapped inside her chest.

"Do you know what I'm going to do?" he asked.

Not with absolute certainty. Dear God, was that the flick of his tongue? He was... Was a gentleman allowed to kiss a woman there?

Her legs quivered, hopelessly unsteady, as his— yes, that was his tongue—daubed against her slit. Embarrassment and excitement warred within her thoughts. It seemed so lewd to be touched like this. To have him kiss and lick and suck her most intimate parts. Oh, but she couldn't stop him. She'd never stop him. Nothing had ever felt so wonderful. Every nerve in her body seemed oversensitive and to be shooting grapeshot that tingled as it reached her skin. Her nipples, that nub of pleasure—was there a word for it?—were all connected. He was batting at it with his tongue so that streamers of fire stretched between all her pleasure points, causing her toes and fingers to curl.

"Sweet devilment, Cora. Promise me you'll be my wife. Say it properly."

Yes! she screamed inwardly, only she was so subsumed by bliss that she couldn't get the actual word out. The blood in her veins became a raging torrent. All her senses lit up, so that Bran became everything, his scent, the touch of his lips and hands. She clasped his hair in her fingers. A firestorm took hold of her cunt. "Oh...oh," she sobbed, while her muscles locked tight, helping her stay upright.

"That's right, my sweet, take this pleasure. Tell the world about it. Shall I always bring you fulfilment first?"

She squealed as she jerked against his mouth.

Cora dragged Bran up off his knees and covered his face with ardent kisses. How could she ever refuse him after that? No one had ever offered her so much pleasure. Lord, now she wanted to return it tenfold.

Cora let her hand slide down his back to his bottom. She smoothed her hands over the back of his tightly-fitted breeches. He had a nicely round cheeks, not too fleshy, but not too muscular either, and with just the right amount of resistance when she dug in her fingertips and squeezed.

"Now let me do the same for you?" She began to bend.

"Dear God, no," he said, stopping her before her mouth came anywhere near his cock. "Save it for our marriage bed."

"I want to give you the same pleasure you've given me."

He made a sound she could only describe as a squeak and she pressed her hand to the hummock beneath his frontfall again. She wanted to see his cock, not just feel it. It seemed so robust, and yet velvety soft. The head, what she could feel of it through his shirttails, was rounded and split like a peach.

"Cora, please."

Was that her taste upon his mouth as he leaned down and kissed her?

"Ho, ho, I think I smell Tink's pomade around here." Lord Swansbrooke's booming voice intruded upon the moment.

Cora immediately stiffened.

"Try the buffet," her cousin, Bennett interjected, his voice laced with the same sycophantic slime it always did when in the presence of anyone with more than half a crown to their name. "She always hid in such places as a child. She used to leave biscuit crumbs out for the elves to find."

"Did it work?" Bran whispered into her ear.

"I fear it only encouraged the mice," Cora murmured. His calmness soothed her a little. Suddenly, the dog-parlour filled with the sounds of raucous laughter, and the yowls and woofs of the woken dogs.

"Straighten your things." Bran released his hold upon her.

Cora fussed with her bodice. He'd torn the stitching loose, so that it didn't sit right, but she covered the damage as best she could with her fichu. She wondered if anyone had yet found Harriet.

The buffet door opened, and Harriet wasn't among the crowd. Lord Swansbrooke and her cousin Bennett reached in and plucked them both out.

"Well now, Cora. I hope you and Mr. Locke weren't getting too acquainted."

Cora clucked. "Mr. Locke and I have known one another since birth, and if you hadn't been so slow, cousin, then I wouldn't have had to spend so long in there. Are we now done with this ridiculous game?"

"Well, by rights we should all squash in beside you."

"I have been quite thoroughly squashed enough, Mr. Ashcroft. I think we may pass on that particular part. What is next? A drink, some dancing, perhaps?"

"There's still Miss Cholmondeley to find."

Cora gave Cousin Bennett a terse nod. "Where have you looked? I last saw her in the yellow drawing room. She won't have gone far." Then without a backward glance, though it killed her not to do so, Cora swept towards the door leading the revellers on their final hunt.

That was surely for the best, she thought. She didn't want any more questions to be asked, and nor did she want to announce her engagement. They'd do that quietly to their families first, in their own time.

Besides, she really did mean for Harriet to win

her hat. She'd have to make that quite clear to Bran.

-4-

MISUNDERSTANDING & MISCONDUCT

"YOU'VE NOT PERSUADED her then?"

Bran watched Cora's rump sway as she disappeared out of the dog-parlour. "You're timing's appalling." He scowled at Hugh, allowing his friend to believe he'd failed. Any announcements he'd make with Cora by his side, and he preferred not to have any speculation circulating beforehand. He rather hoped that was why Cora had run off too. They'd set their own pace with this, not have society dictate it to them because they'd been found together.

Swansbrooke settled himself before the hearth, with a dog or two piled around his feet. "I didn't care for the speculation that had started brewing. Bennett has a vile tongue on him." He drew his brows low over his beetle-black eyes. "I know you mean to do right by her, Tink, but you have to take care of a woman's reputation. They have to be nurtured, because if there's so much as a whiff of scandal they end up with as much respect as a barnacle's whisker."

"What was Bennett saying?"

"Only that it was curious you were the only ones not to be found, and that most likely we would find the three of you together, for Harriet and Cora are bosom friends, and you're often known to collar a brace of ducks."

"Little twit. What in heavens does he hope to achieve in insinuating that?"

"To ensure he gets a whiff at the inheritance, that's what. By ruining her reputation and scaring all the good men off. He thinks like everyone else that your proposition earlier was mere jest. If Cora increases then Reeve's more likely to leave it to his grandson than his clod of a nephew. But she can't beget if her reputation is in tatters. No one will want her."

"I want her." Dear God, he still had the taste of her upon his lips. Those few stolen moments they'd shared weren't nearly enough. He looked around the room at the tatty wall coverings and the overflowing grate full of ash, half hoping that if he waited a few moments she'd come back. Of course, she didn't.

Squeals of laughter from across the hall suggested that Miss Cholmondeley had been found, and now the revellers were returning to their earlier pursuits, predominately drinking, with a bit of sociable chatter thrown in for good measure.

"I have to have more time alone with her, Hugh."

Hugh shuffled his feet. Then he leaned forward to pet the head of the dog that he'd disturbed. "Don't be ridiculous. It'll look awkward you paying her that much attention in one night."

"I don't care if I raise suspicions. I'm planning on marrying her, for Lord's sake."

"Yes, but it's not seemly to appear overly fond of one's wife, even before the wedding. What you need to do is stay away from her for a bit. Allow your humours to settle, and offer her some space. If she's genuinely interested, then she'll come to you. Be the light, Tink, instead of the moth. That way you'll not get burned."

Bran put his hand to his mouth and plucked at his lips. The notion didn't suit him at all. Why would he marry her if he didn't want to spend every moment worshipping her? If he wanted a fair weather friend, then maintaining a mistress would be an altogether less expensive affair than supporting a wife.

"Are you describing Miss Reeve as a moth?" he asked, by way of a half-hearted attempted at humour. Clearly, he still sounded too peevish, because Lord Swansbrooke frowned.

"A butterfly," he reassured, smacking Bran encouragingly across the back, "but a fair single-minded one. I'll give you that you've not chosen a dainty being to offer up your heart to. However, you Tinker, are most definitely a moth. It's all that brown and buff you favour that does it. I shouldn't be surprised if Miss Reeve doesn't find you a little fusty. You ought to think about that. Even your choice of seduction venue is of a similar bent. Now your dear, see she is quite the opposite of fusty."

Bran scratched his head. The brightest article in

his wardrobe was a peacock blue coat he wore to observe the races, for the primary purpose of standing out so that he could be seen by his friends in the crowd. Cora by comparison favoured deep Veronese green, or scarlet, mixed with rich, striking brocades. He expressed his flamboyance in his actions. Clothes served only to keep one warm. But if Hugh thought it mattered, he supposed he could try the peacock blue at breakfast. Assuming his man had packed it.

Meanwhile, if he meant to avoid drawing attention, then he ought to take himself to his chamber for the night, for if he saw the slightest opportunity to do so, he'd have Cora in a cupboard again in a trice.

~ * ~

Cora couldn't understand it. Yes, she'd fronted the group to search for Harriet, but that had simply been to draw the attention away from the fact she'd been discovered in a broom closet with a man of non-filial acquaintance. That and she'd had to fake a fall to account for the situation with her dress. Bran had not only torn the stitching holding her bodice in place, he'd also knocked her stomacher skew-whiff and left a red mark upon her neck.

Despite her staged fall, her mama remained curiously po-faced. Cora didn't think her convinced. No, her mama seemed deeply suspicious. Although by nature she was a twitchy little mouse. Actually, more of a shrew than a mouse. Only the presence of

Aunt Tessa had prevented one of her horrid whispered attacks, in which she sounded utterly reasonable but dripped vitriol beneath her breath. As it was, she'd given Cora a vicious pinch—warning perhaps, not to further misbehave.

If only the opportunity for further unseemly conduct would present itself. Where the devil was the ridiculous man? For someone who'd been so recently driven to express his utmost regard for her person, he was now failing to instil a sense of confidence in his long-term loyalty.

She'd said yes and now he was nowhere to be found.

It wouldn't suit, if Bran turned out to be the flighty sort. She wanted long term loyalty and faithfulness. Assuming such a thing did in fact exist. The whole world knew Aunt Tessa shared her father's bed. Aunt Tessa had lived with him and mama for nigh on twenty years, which Cora supposed in part accounted for her mama's frightfully spiteful nature.

Bran had understood that she'd said yes, hadn't he? She'd said it to him as they kissed, and though she hadn't replied when he'd asked her again, while he was nestled between her thighs, he surely must have known that she agreed.

"Miss Reeve, are you feeling well? You seem distracted."

Cora steadied herself against the Chinois-style sideboard and then handed her companion her half-drunk glass. "I'm fine, Lord Egremont. I fear that it is just the hour grown late."

"Aye, it is that. And many are weary. I've just seen Tinker Locke strolling about in his night cap. Seems Hulme has already found another soul to share the cot they were paired for, so he was seeking a berth with Lord Swansbrooke. Perhaps, we all ought to consider our beds. Meaning you no disrespect, my dear, of course."

Meaning to assure her that he wasn't thinking of her in her night-rail, or sprawled across his bed. If Bran had retired, were such images prominent in his thoughts?

"Indeed, I think you are right, and I shall do just that. Good night, Lord Egremont."

Why hadn't she considered that Bran might have retired? Perhaps because she'd been too distracted by her mother's pinch. It was all too easy to suppose the frightful woman had somehow seen him off. She probably thought Bran too lowly to make her a good match, failing to see anything of significance besides status and wealth. Cora well understood her mother's thoughts, hence Lord Egremont's stint at her side tonight.

From the corner of her eye Cora spied Lord Swansbrooke. With that enormous beak of a nose he was rather hard to miss. He sat at the whist table with her father, Aunt Tessa, the Lovichs and Samuel de Motte, which meant Bran was all alone upstairs, and more importantly she now knew where to go to seek him out. While the allocation of the rooms was a fiercely guarded secret, she knew perfectly well that Lord Swansbrooke, as the highest ranking guest, had been given the very best room, namely, the Walnut Suite, which lay a mere hop across the corridor from her room.

"Goodnight, Papa. I'm going to retire now." He gave her a rather significant look, as if he'd expected her to say something more insightful than that. Cora shook her head at him, whilst his stare tied her tongue in a knot.

"All right, my dear," he said eventually. He gave a sigh and waved her off, laying down his card to show he had won both the trick and the rubber. So his discontent had to be directed at her and not his gambling fortune. Heavens, was he disappointed with her? Had he expected word of her engagement? Surely the news of Bran's first proposal and her refusal had already reached him. Perhaps it was that her mother or Cousin Bennett brought tidings of her misdemeanour? The latter had probably elaborated upon her discovery in the buffet with a man she'd turned down only hours before.

No, if father had been concerned over her conduct, he'd have dragged Bran before him and made him reiterate that offer for her hand, or else had him ejected from the house. She clucked her tongue. Perhaps this once, Bennett had actually held his tongue.

That still didn't allay her fears that Bran hadn't understood her, and she did so very much want to see him again. Surely one grand gesture deserved another.

Cora veered right at the head of the stairs.

Hadn't Aunt Tessa said at the start of the season

that she ought to make absolutely sure her prospective life mate could satisfy her before she made a commitment, for there was no undoing it after the marriage act? She didn't suppose Tessa had intended quite such an interpretation as this, but then knowing Tessa, mayhap she had.

She was going to find Bran and make sure he knew exactly how much she wanted him. He'd stopped her earlier, but she wouldn't be thwarted now. She'd return the pleasure he'd given her. That's how she wanted their marriage to be, based on at least some notion of equality.

Sex. Tupping. Fornication. The words ran through her head with accompanying pictures as she walked along the corridor. She'd do this so that he knew just how ardently she wished him to take her to wife.

Only the odd murmur seeped beneath of the doors of the chambers nearest the grand stairs. Further into the east wing, not even candlelight glowed beneath the doorframes. Cora put her hand on her dressing room door, but rather than enter and pass-through into the bedchamber beyond she hastily looked about. The door to the Walnut Suite lay only a few yards away, just down the step that led into the oldest part of the house. Quietly she crept along the edge of the carpet runner. Lord, this was probably a hopelessly bad idea, but she had to express to Bran how she felt.

No reply came in response to her tap. "Mr. Locke, Bran?" she hissed through the latch. Pray God he wasn't asleep yet. She raised her hand again and knocked a little louder. "Bran, are you there? It's Cora." Oh, darn fiddlesticks with this, she raised the latch. The room lay in shadows broken only by the soft glowing embers in the grate. "Bran?" she hissed, not daring to raise her voice. She tiptoed right up to the bed, which owing to the curtains lay in total darkness. She reached out, seeking the wild tangle of his overlong forelock upon the pillow, but to her immense disappointment found only empty space. Perhaps, Lord Egremont had been wrong, and Bran wasn't bedded here at all.

~ * ~

Bran emerged from the privy to a sight that had him so stumped he very nearly back stepped into the potty. "Cora?" She didn't seem to hear him. Her slender apparition stood poised beside the bed, blond ringlets wreathed by the golden glow from the embers of the fire. Her body inclined over the bed, where she had one hand pressed to the pillow as if were stroking an imaginary head.

She was every inch lovely, and he wanted every bit of her in his bed. Dear Lord how he wanted her in his bed. His body responded at once. Heat rushed to his groin and his cock rose like mast drawn aloft.

She'd come to seek him out, he realised, which surely meant she felt the same way. Joy followed the flood of arousal, making him feel impossibly light, although the wild flutter of his pulse kept his tongue in check a moment longer. "Cora."

She heard him that second time, for she turned so abruptly she had to put out a hand to steady herself. Bran met her where she stood, her hand clamped tight around the bed post. A myriad of questions flooded his thoughts. Why was she here? For what purpose? To seek him? For something else?

In the end, he asked only the most pertinent of the lot. "Are you looking for Lord Swansbrooke?" It would be typical of his god-awful luck if she turned out to be the one woman in all of old England that actually turned doe-eyed at the thought of caressing Hugh's domineering snout.

"I was looking for you," she said, clearly petted at his insinuation. "Why would I seek Lord Swansbrooke?"

"I thought only... This is his room." He tried to keep the accusation from his voice.

"I know that."

"But you're here."

She smiled, and the plumpness it added to her cheeks made the glow in his heart warm. "I overheard that you'd been forced to swap." Yes, he'd been about ready to murder Hulme for that about forty minutes ago, but now he thought he might actually shake his hand. There'd have been no Cora visiting his bedside if he'd been bedded down with that lecherous fox.

"Yes...um... I was." Bran fanned his arms out, suddenly conscious that he stood before her only in his nightshirt, with nothing beneath and a full half of his legs on display down to the skin. His toes curled into the soft pile of the carpet. Egremont had definitely given Hugh his best room. He wasn't accustomed to carpet underfoot, just the normal creaking, cold wooden boards.

The same observation regarding his near nakedness seemed to strike Cora at that moment too, for her gaze lingered over his body. "Why did you not wait for me, but chose instead to retire?"

He thought he detected a flush colouring her cheeks, but it was deuced impossible to be certain in this light. Bran found a spill and lit the candle by the bedstead, then another that he set upon the chest at the foot-end. "You were in such a rush to depart after we were found that it seemed best not to pursue you. Also, Lord Swansbrooke advised me against making another scene. Apparently more than one in a night smacks of desperation, which is not appealing I'm told."

"Are you desperate for me?" The little romp grinned as if she already knew the answer was yes.

"I'm..." He was what exactly? What was he going to admit? That beneath this flimsy slip he was purse-proud at the prospect of having her lie in his arms? That he couldn't get the thoughts of their earlier tête à tête out of his head? That he wanted her above all else, right now, here in this enormous beast of a bed? He'd been so sorely used this evening that he'd been contemplating an assignment with Miss Rosie and her four sisters tonight. "Cora, I'm besotted. I've asked you twice. Must I make that thrice before you'll accept me?" He came to her and took her hands in his, raising them to press kisses to her knuckles.

"I've already said yes. Did you not hear me?"

"But you didn't scream it out as I asked."

"I'm afraid I was finding it a little difficult to stand, let alone to express any sort of coherent verbal response. I came looking for you because I want to return that favour."

"You want to what?" Good God, was she serious? He couldn't let her do that.

"I want to please you. You will tell me what you need and let me do that, won't you, Bran? I simply couldn't endure the thought of you treating me like a doll and seeking your pleasures elsewhere because you were afraid of breaking me."

Bran nudged up her chin with his fingertips so he could look into her eyes. She was serious. He had no doubt of it. This only confirmed that she was absolutely the right choice. Most of the women he'd encountered cared only to know that a gentleman had a haberdasher's account and a surplus of coins in the bank. Cora—his love—wanted to ensure she satisfied his physical needs.

"We ought to wait," he said. "Until we're married."

She drew her teeth over her lower lip. "How should anybody know that we've done otherwise? I shan't tell them, and Lord Swansbrooke is engaged at the card table. Besides, how is it different to what you did earlier?"

That one had him stumped. "Cora," he pleaded. Did she have any concept of how much this conversation was killing him? He wanted very much to let her do exactly as she asked, and to let his rigid cock fill up her sweet mouth.

"I want to touch you." She swept aside his hands and grasped immediately at his nightshirt, her hot little hands folding tightly around his waist. "I only felt the shape of you earlier."

His cock immediately bucked in welcome. "Bolt the door."

Cora did so at once.

Bran removed his shift while her back was turned and readied himself for her shock. He knew she'd never seen a naked man before.

To his relief, she didn't scream or giggle, nor make any motion that suggested she might faint. Instead her gaze focussed sharply upon him and ran down from his head to his shoulders and chest and then stopped at his loins. Her lips parted slightly, and the very tip of her tongue swept over her lower lip.

"Do you still wish to kiss me there?" he breathed.

She drew closer with her hand outstretched. Bran's eyes closed for a second as her hand made contact with his cock. The fan of lace bordering her sleeve scraped across his skin, providing a fraction more stimulation than he really liked. Bran's ballocks pulled up tight against the shield of his body.

She didn't move at first, simply held him cocooned in the palm of her hand.

"Like this." He wrapped his hand over the top of hers and showed her how to stroke him. She bit her lip all the while, concentrating hard upon the act until her breath released in a great gush.

Bran slid his hands up her back and pulled her fast against his chest. He sought her lips and a dance made of kisses. Cora opened up to him, but her hand never left his shaft. "Does it please you to touch me like this?" he asked.

"I like the way it makes your words catch. If I keep up the caress will you reach a peak similar to the one I had earlier?"

Cora snuck a glance down at him. He stood proudly upright, the tip of his cock drumming against the skin just shy of his navel. His foreskin was drawn back so that the sensitive flare of the head lay exposed, and blood pumped through it like licks of fire.

"Yes," he whispered into her ear, "but it'll be a lot stickier, and it will take me a while to recover. Do you still wish to kiss me there?"

He felt her tremble against his arm.

"You don't have to, Cora. I won't demand anything you're not ready to give."

"But it would please you if I did?" Her eyes shone a little too bright.

"You please me," he said, backing up a little. He sat on the edge of the bed holding her hands.

"Maybe a little taste."

Bran's stomach muscles tensed. His cock swelled at the very thought of her kiss. He watched her sink slowly onto her knees so that her voluminous dress fanned around her. Slowly, cautiously, she bent her head towards his lap. Bran placed a hand upon her shoulder. "Cora." Her name emerged from his throat as a croak.

"I want to do this, Bran."

Damn, she near intoxicated him. Her mouth opened slightly, so he could see the rose shadow of her tongue. Then her lips met with his shaft, causing him to claw at the bedspread with both hands. She really was magnificent and soon to be truly his.

She explored him with her lips to begin with, and then with the very tip of her tongue. That was devilment enough as she directed her attention to the sensitive crown of his cock, where she soon learned to lap up the pearls of seed he wept.

He stopped her short of taking him fully into her mouth. "Cora, don't." He couldn't take it. Already, she'd worn his restraint down to a thread. The heat of her mouth, combined with delicate tugging sucks would send him over the edge, and he didn't want that. Not yet. First he wanted her. "I need to be hard if we're to tup," he blurted, not really intending to say it aloud, even though it was the primary thought in his brain.

~ * ~

"If we're to tup."

Just the sound of his husky voice as he spoke the words made her insides flutter. Cora stared up at him. She knew it was rude to stare, but she'd never really caught so much as a glimpse of a cock before tonight and it was... well, it was magnificent. All straight and proud and stout, and yet so warm and supple beneath her touch and pulsing with vitality. The taste of him sat thick upon her tongue.

"I'm sorry," he apologized. "I didn't mean to say that."

"I wish you'd lit more candles. I can barely see you in this light," she replied, avoiding the issue. Lord help her, though she trembled, she knew the moment he said it that she wanted him—them—to do just that. She wanted him to tup her.

"Two is illumination enough." He forced a chuckle, which caused his shaft to quiver and jerk. Then his stomach muscles rippled as he dragged down another breath. "I know you heard me, Cora. If you don't want us to do that, then you ought to leave now, because if you stay I'll interpret that as a yes."

"I know that I shouldn't."

"You shouldn't be here at all."

She knew that too. However, they both knew she wasn't going to leave. The silence between them stretched. Finally, Bran bent and pressed his lips to her breast. He undid the temporary repair to her dress and worked the top of her stays loose so that he could once again free her breasts.

The memory of his earlier touch flooded back to her as he sucked upon her nipples.

"Bran, would you kiss me as you did before?"

"Kiss you?" He raised his head. "Is that not what I'm doing?"

"As before." She dipped her head so that he would understand that she wanted him to kiss between her legs again.

"Ah," he laughed. "Then we best swap positions." Without preamble, he settled her upon the edge of the mattress. Whereupon, he removed her shoes and kissed the arch of her foot. "Lie back." Bran loomed over her, naked, his muscles taut and pleasingly shadowed in the firelight. His body continued to amaze her. He was not soft or rounded in any place save for his rump. No, rather he was pleasingly different, and so very very male.

He braced one hand by the side of her head, and used the other to explore the contours of her leg to high above her stocking top. The action made her limbs jelly-like, making her glad of the mattress at her back. It was the work of a moment for him to tuck up her skirt between them, so that she was spread like a banquet for him, with her cork rump pushing her hips up and out. Bran spread her thighs, and brought his mouth to her cunt.

Her breasts trembled along with the rest of her as his tongue tickled the edge of her folds. When he flicked lightly over the pip that was the focus of her tingling pleasure, she nearly sat upright on the bed, the sensation was so intense. Instead, she bunched the bedspread in her fists and tried to stifle the keening wail that rose from her throat. "Don't stop," she pleaded when he lifted his head a moment.

Bran smiled up at her from beneath the wild tangle of his fringe. She couldn't see much of his eyes, only enough to realise they were dark with intent. His mouth pulled tight into a devilish smile.

"I've no intention of ever stopping, but you know this is really just a little preparation for the main act." He gave her another sly lick then made a pillow of her thigh. A moment later, his fingers replaced the flick of his tongue, brushing through her wiry golden curls and up and over her nub.

"Oh," she gasped. He began circling with his thumb, so that it felt as though a thread were drawn tight and her very being was being bunched into that one tight spot. Just when she thought her crisis was surely about to drown her in its swell, Bran eased his fingers into the picture. One then two slipped inside her. He didn't press too deeply, a fact that after a few strokes made her writhe all the wilder. Her body craved more, her sheath clutched at his fingers, trying to drag him in.

Surely this was it, the moment when he'd enter her. She didn't think she'd ever be more ready than this, though the thought of such intimacy still made her tremble and her chest lock tight.

"Cora," he sighed her name then slid upwards and covered her body. He fit himself neatly against her puss. Lord, the blessed heat of him. His cock felt satin smooth and enormous.

How could this possibly work?

"Say it, Cora. Tell me how much you want me."

He was all tension, tendons straining like corded steel, and yet so silky against her flesh.

"Say it," he urged, more than a little panic peppering his voice.

Damn if she wasn't half-terrified, but this was what she'd wanted. Still wanted. She closed her eyes, and gripped the sweat-slicked muscles of his shoulders. "I want you to do this." She spoke the words directly between his lips. "Please, come inside."

It sounded so tart and silly, but if Bran thought her words odd, he didn't have the breath to comment. The air whistled through his lips, while he fit their bodies neatly together in one smooth push.

Oh, my! A shocked gasp forced its way out of her mouth. He was... Dear lord, could she tolerate it? He was inside of her, and she couldn't keep still.

Cora knew every part of him in that moment, the shape of him, the contours, the way he was forcing her to make room for his cock. And jolting inside her as the walls of her sheath clung to him.

It felt strange... and oh, her body began to relax, and the push wasn't so fierce, but rather more of a glide, and she wanted more of him and deeper. As deep as he could go, even though there was an edge of pain to the process. "More," she whimpered, when he held back after one of her more voluble gasps.

"Are you sure? I'm not hurting you, am I?" He lifted his weight from her, so that his hands lay braced either side of her shoulders.

"Only a very tiny amount."

His face clouded immediately.

"But I like it. I want you to continue," she immediately added. No, she most definitely wasn't going to let him stop.

"All right, Cora. But I'd like you to know how

much this is killing me." A trickle of sweat rolled down the side of his temples, and for the first time she noticed the front of his hair was wet. "You're so tight. You're gripping me. It's so hard not to just push. Don't move, now, not an inch."

She held herself impossibly still, while peering down through the gap between their bodies so that she could see where his flesh locked with hers. How intimate. What a glorious sight. But she wanted him to move.

"Gad," he whistled. "I said not an inch."

"But Bran, I want you deeper."

He made a sort of croaking sound and then sank down onto her, crushing her in his grip, before rolling them over so that he lay on his back with her astride his hips. "Right, now you can control it." He gave her a little push, so that she sat above him rather than being cuddled up close. "But slowly. Slow and steady, all right."

Slow and steady, she repeated in her head. As if she were about to rush such a thing. There was still a borderline twinge of pain if she pushed too far in a certain direction, but then after a few strokes a sort of numbness dulled the edge of that, and things became altogether far more slick and pleasurable.

Bran reached out to her and started making circles around her nub, which brought a double layer of heat to her cheeks. His touch was so intimate, and he surely could feel the very point where they were joined. Her insides began to flutter at the notion of reaching down and touching that point herself.

Instead, she stroked the coarse patch of hair upon his chest. Every part of his body was so new and unfamiliar. His irises were all smoke-coloured now, and far brighter than they'd been earlier in the night.

"Damn," he said when she tweaked hard upon one of his tiny yet robust nipples. The word was a soft explosion unto its self. "You don't know how damn sweet..." He closed his eyes and breathed deeply through his nose before looking up at her again. "How desperately I really want to fuck."

She might not understand precisely, but she did recognise the tension eating up his body, so that every muscle seemed locked tight, apart from the one connecting them, which bowed and flexed. And she could only assume, since they were already bound, that he meant to take things up a pace.

"I've got to," he said, thrusting up so that he raised his hips and then slapped them back down. "Just got to."

The shock of the furious motion sent Cora reeling. She fell head first into a blissful squall. Her limbs twitched. She had no control over the motion, none at all. Each part of her seemed independent of the rest, though all dancing to the same impossible, pounding, thumping beat.

Bran's beat.

Bran's fingers, his hips, were the controlling forces as he ushered her along to a blinding climax. Already the spring coiled within her abdomen was wound overly tight. When Bran thrust harder, it seemed to unwind all at once.

Cora collapsed into a long shuddering madness from which there was no escape. She'd never felt anything like it, not even during her earlier peak. Having him deep inside her, still sliding back and forth with a momentum that made their bodies slap together so loudly it was surely audible in the corridor, made the moment all the more intense.

Her muscles fluttered and flexed. The bedstead groaned beneath them. Cora hid her face against Bran's neck, all the while aware of the rapidity of his pulse. He held himself tight and still as his cock made what turned out to be its final pulse.

In the quiet that followed, she lay very still, hardly daring to breathe. Bran continued to hold her snug against his body. The sound of his heartbeat thundered in her ears. She'd never really thought beyond this point to what came next. Would he truly expect her to trip back across the hall? What did they do when Swansbrooke knocked upon the door?

Bran tilted his head towards hers, until their brows lay pressed together. "Cora Reeve, I know I've asked and you say that you've answered before, but I'm going to ask you again regardless. Will you do me the honour of becoming my wife?"

Who the hell cared what happened next? "Yes, oh yes please. I will, you wicked and delicious man, but we can't say so yet." She smacked a kiss down hard upon his lips to silence his questions. "I don't want to win the bet, you see. If I do, Charlotte will never speak to either of us again."

"Can't have that."

"And I do so want Harriet to win."

Bran frowned, and then he tucked her more firmly against his shoulder. "Let's see how long it takes for us to be caught. Until then, you have my silence, and my heart. Though, I swear I also intend to tup you at every opportunity."

Cora nudged her elbow into his ribs. "Then we'd both best set to work on finding Harriet a husband."

"How about Hugh?"

"Lord Swansbrooke?"

"He's a very big heart."

"And an even larger nose. I don't know, Bran. Harriet is so petite, and she hasn't really anything to offer him. Her dowry isn't all it could be."

Bran merely closed his eyes and smiled. "They sound like a perfect match. We'll arrange it. When we're not tupping, that is." And he rolled over on top of her so that he pressed her into the mattress. "Right now, I think we need more practice. I do know how you like to be the very best at everything."

Cora welcomed his kiss. She didn't doubt that under Bran's tuition, she'd excel at bedsports in no time.

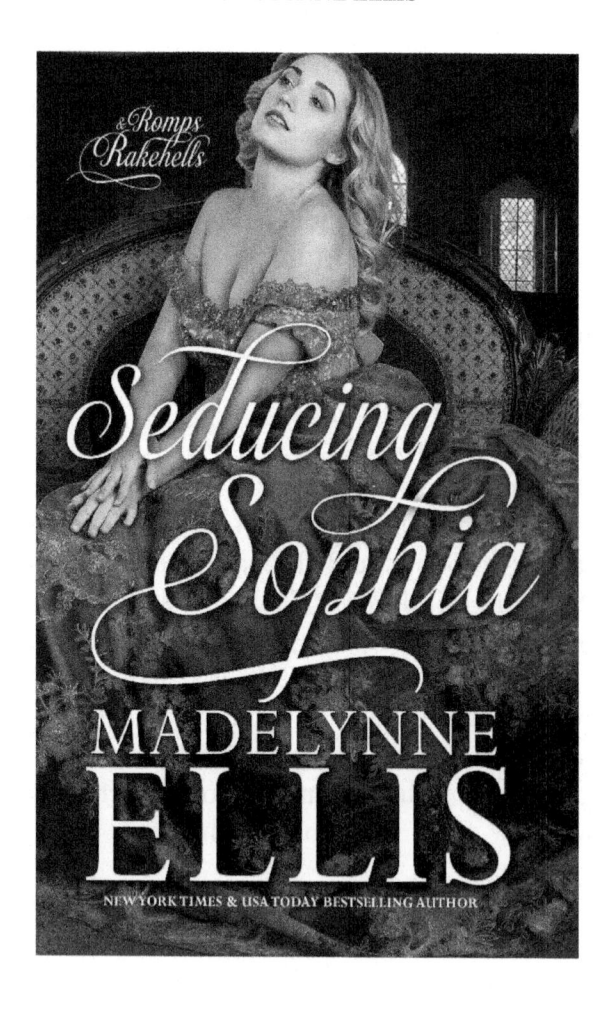

Paris Ashcroft supports himself by offering discreet sexual liaisons to women whose husbands neglect their duties. However, when Sophia Lovich—the woman he's lost his heart to—seeks his affections he's caught up in a web of passion between a husband and wife.

Taming Taylor

Madelynne Ellis

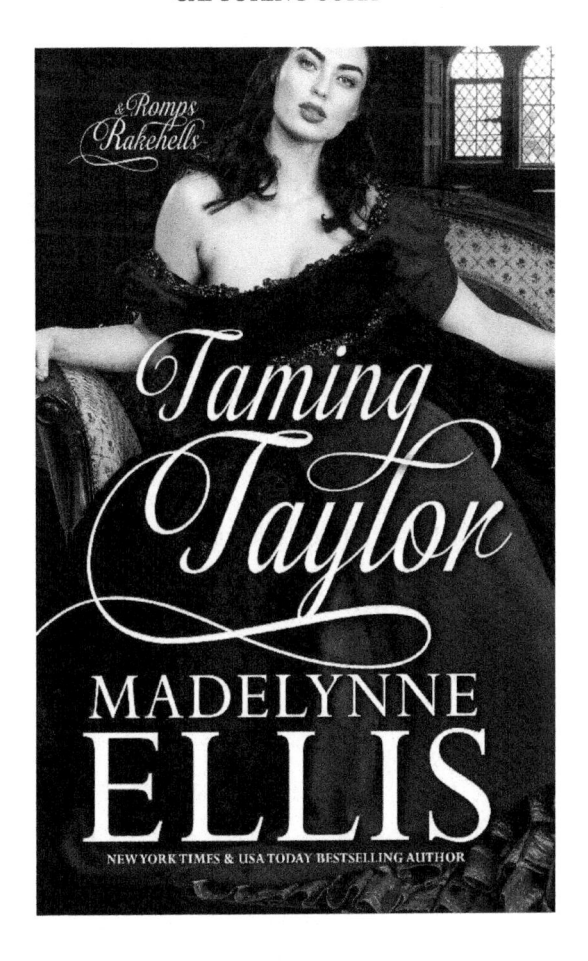

NEW YORK TIMES & USA TODAY BESTSELLING AUTHOR

Consummate rakehell, Taylor Hulme has two passions in life, extravagant clothes and buxom women. Just as he's never without a spare coat, he keeps two lovers in case the first cannot satisfy his needs. Naturally, he takes utmost care to ensure they never meet.

When they accidentally do, the two women combine forces determined to teach Taylor the error of his ways.

-about the author-

Madelynne Ellis lives in the UK, not far from the Welsh border with her partner, family, & assorted pets. She is currently sipping rapidly cooling decaf coffee while listening to loud music, & indulging her obsession for tattooed bad boys.

Connect with her in the following places:

www.madelynne-ellis.com

madelynne@madelynne-ellis.com

Printed in Great Britain
by Amazon